"HELLO READING books are a perfect introduction to reading. Brief sentences full of word repetition and full-color pictures stress visual clues to help a child take the first important steps toward reading. Mastering these storybooks will build children's reading confidence and give them the enthusiasm to stand on their own in the world of words."

—Bee Cullinan
Past President of the International Reading
Association, Professor in New York University's
Early Childhood and Elementary Education Program

"Readers aren't born, they're made. Desire is planted—planted by parents who work at it."

—Jim Trelease
author of *The Read-Aloud Handbook*

"When I was a classroom reading teacher, I recognized the importance of good stories in making children understand that reading is more than just recognizing words. I saw that children who have ready access to storybooks get excited about reading. They also make noticeably greater gains in reading comprehension. The development of the HELLO READING stories grows out of this experience."

—Harriet Ziefert
M.A.T., New York University School of Education
Author, Language Arts Module,
Scholastic Early Childhood Program

For Jeff
—S.M.

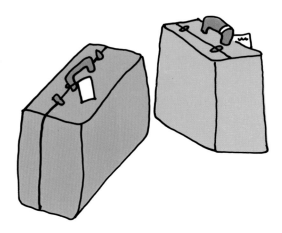

PUFFIN BOOKS
Published by the Penguin Group
Viking Penguin, a division of Penguin Books USA Inc.,
40 West 23rd Street, New York, New York 10010, U.S.A.
Penguin Books Ltd, 27 Wrights Lane, London W8 5TZ, England
Penguin Books Australia Ltd, Ringwood, Victoria, Australia
Penguin Books Canada Ltd, 2801 John Street, Markham, Ontario, Canada L3R 1B4
Penguin Books (N.Z.) Ltd, 182–190 Wairau Road, Auckland 10, New Zealand

Penguin Books Ltd, Registered Offices: Harmondsworth, Middlesex, England

Published in Puffin Books, 1990

1 3 5 7 9 10 8 6 4 2
Text copyright © Harriet Ziefert, 1990
Illustrations copyright © Suzy Mandel, 1990
All rights reserved

Library of Congress Catalog Card Number: 89-62904
ISBN: 0-14-054222-1

Printed in Singapore for Harriet Ziefert, Inc.

Tim and Jim Take Off

Harriet Ziefert
Pictures by Suzy Mandel

PUFFIN BOOKS

"Here we are!" said Mom.
"We're at the airport."

"Yippee!" said Tim.
"Yippee!" said Jim.

They went to check in.

A man checked tickets.
He checked bags, too.

A woman checked Tim and Jim.
She checked everything and
everyone going to the gate.

Tim and Jim said good-bye
to their mother at the gate.

They walked onto the plane.
They looked into the cockpit.

A flight attendant said,
"Sit down.
Buckle your seat belts.
I'll put away your backpacks."

"I'm excited," said Tim.
"I'm scared," said Jim.
"Me, too!" said Tim.

Soon it was time for takeoff.

The plane sped down the runway and...

soon it was in the air!

The pilot turned off
the seat belt sign.

Tim and Jim went for a walk
to see the inside of the plane.

They saw the galley…

and the exit doors...

and the bathroom.

"I smell food," said Tim.
"So do I," said Jim.

So they walked back
to their seats.

A flight attendant brought the food.

Tim ate an apple...
and rolls...
but not the beans!

Jim ate salad...
and rolls...
but not the beans!

Tim fell asleep.

Jim read.
He read a book.
He read the safety card.
He read what it said
on the "throw-up" bag.

Jim woke Tim up.
The pilot said,
"We'll soon be on the ground.

The temperature is 86°.
The skies are clear.
Thank you for flying with us."

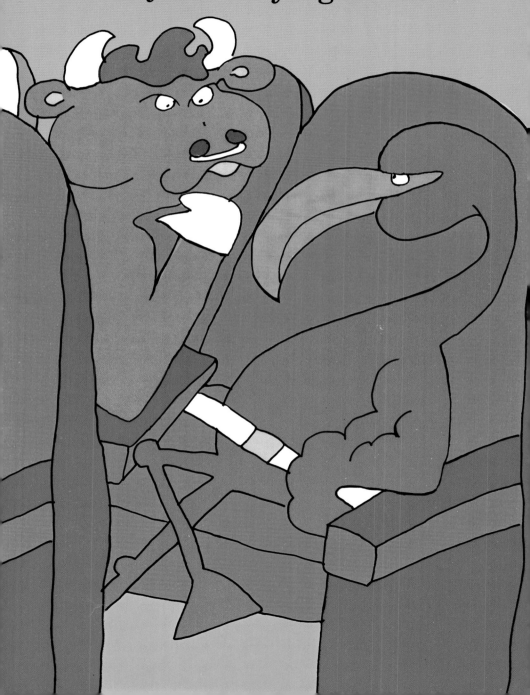

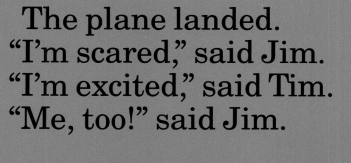

The plane landed.
"I'm scared," said Jim.
"I'm excited," said Tim.
"Me, too!" said Jim.

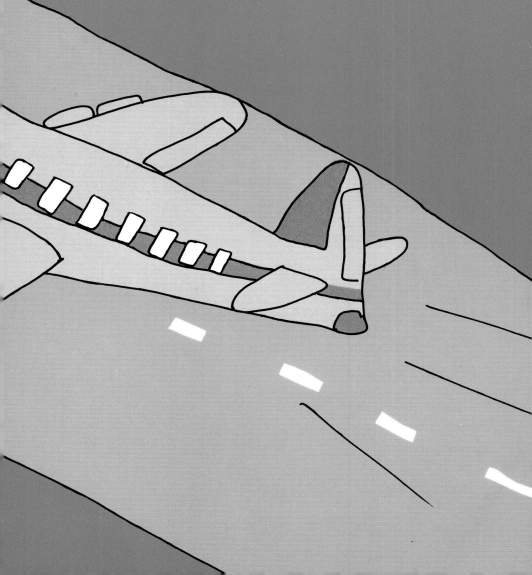

The plane came to a full stop.
Tim and Jim got their backpacks.

They walked down the steps.
They walked to the gate.

"Hi, Grandma!"
"Hi, Grandpa!"